The Silly Sisters

By Dave Werner
Illustrated by Lucinda McQueen

*For Leah and Margot, and
with special thanks to Cary—D.W.*

A GOLDEN BOOK • NEW YORK

Western Publishing Company, Inc., Racine, Wisconsin 53404

A B C D E F G H I J K L M

Lulu Mouse had light brown hair. Mimi Mouse
had dark brown hair. Lulu was six. Mimi was
just five and a half, but she was as tall as Lulu.
They lived next door to each other, and they were
the best of friends. When they were together,
everything they said and did was funny.

Lulu and Mimi liked to wear the same kind of clothes.

Sometimes they liked to wear the same clothes at the same time!

On rainy days they stayed inside and painted pictures. One day Mimi painted a picture of Lulu with a million-billion rainbows. Lulu painted a picture of Mimi with a billion-zillion hearts.

When they showed the pictures to their mothers,
Lulu's mother said, "Who's who? These look like
pictures of two sisters."

"You two do look enough alike to be sisters,"
said Mimi's mother.

The two little mice thought that was very funny.

Lulu and Mimi went to look in the mirror to see
for themselves. Then they began making scary
faces until they got too scared. They giggled and
giggled.

"Making scary faces is hard work," said Lulu. "I'm tired."

"Me, too," agreed Mimi. "Let's yawn together."

"OK," said Lulu. "Ready?"

"Ready," answered Mimi.

Together they counted, "One, two, three, YAAAAWWWNNN!"

They giggled so hard, they had to sit down.

On days when Lulu had lunch at Mimi's house, she didn't eat cheese because Mimi didn't eat cheese.

And when Mimi ate lunch at Lulu's house, she didn't drink berry juice because Lulu didn't drink berry juice.

"You two are so silly," said Lulu's mother with a grin.

"We're just like sisters," said Lulu.

"We're just like sisters," repeated Mimi.

Then they both started giggling.

"The Silly Sisters," said Lulu's father. "That's what we'll call you."

"We're the Silly Sisters!" shrieked the two little mice.

One day at Mimi's house the Silly Sisters decided to play exercise class. They wore matching blue leotards and sparkly pink tights.

"First we s-t-r-e-t-c-h," said Lulu as she reached up high.

"S-t-r-e-t-c-h," repeated Mimi, also reaching up high.

Lulu had brought her tape recorder and some dance music. It was very loud and the beat was very fast.

"Now we touch our toes," said Lulu. "One-two-three-four, one-two-three-four."

The music went faster and faster. Lulu said, faster and faster, "Onetwothreefour, onetwothreefour—"

Mimi could not keep up with her. "Wait, wait!" she cried. As she reached for her toes she felt herself bump hard against Lulu.

"OUCH!" cried Lulu. She pushed Mimi away. "OUCH!" cried Mimi, landing on the floor with a thud.

"Mommy!" said Mimi, sobbing. "Lulu pushed me!"

"I'm going home right now," cried Lulu. She ran for the door. "I don't want to be your silly old sister!"

"Fine!" yelled Mimi through her tears. "I don't want to be your silly old sister, either!"

The next day Lulu stayed home alone. She searched her closet for something to wear—something different from anything Mimi had. She found an old dress she had outgrown. It looked funny, but she wore it anyway.

"I'd rather look weird than look like Mimi," Lulu told her mother.

Later Lulu drew a picture of herself, but it reminded her of Mimi. She crossed it out and drew some rainbows.

"What beautiful rainbows," Lulu's father said. "But what's this?" He pointed to the crossed-out picture.

"Nothing," muttered Lulu. "It's just a mistake. I'm tired of drawing anyway." Lulu yawned, but she wasn't tired. She was bored.

"I think I'll listen to some music," she said. Then Lulu remembered that she had left her tape recorder at Mimi's house.

Meanwhile, Mimi had invited her friend Heather
Chipmunk to come over for the afternoon.
    At lunch Heather ate two helpings of cheese.
"This is yummy!" she said.
    Mimi wasn't hungry.

They went to Mimi's room. Heather nearly
tripped over something.

"Oh! That's Lulu's tape recorder!" exclaimed
Mimi.

"Who's Lulu?" asked Heather.

"Never mind," said Mimi. "Hey! Let's make
scary faces in the mirror."

"That's dumb," said Heather. "Let's watch
TV instead."

Mimi yawned, but she wasn't tired. She
was bored.

At the breakfast table the next morning Mimi fiddled with Lulu's tape recorder. "Mommy, will you please take Lulu's tape recorder back to her?"

"You want *me* to go see Lulu?" said Mimi's mother. "I thought you two were just like sisters."

Mimi pouted at the tape recorder.

"Why don't you just tell her you're sorry? I'll bet she's sorry, too," said her mother.

"I...just...can't..." said Mimi in a tiny voice. Her finger slipped and turned on the very loud music.

"Turn that off!" said her mother. Then she said, "That tape recorder gives me an idea...."

Lulu heard a knock at her back door. She heard someone calling, "Lulu, Lulu." It sounded like Mimi!

When she opened the door, she was surprised to see no one there. Then she noticed her tape recorder on the step. Instead of music, Mimi's voice was playing. It said, "Here is your tape recorder. I'm sorry. Are you sorry, too?"

Lulu smiled. Mimi was so silly!
Just then Mimi popped out from behind a
nearby bush. Lulu ran over and hugged Mimi. The
two little mice jumped up and down—and giggled.

Lulu's father came to the door. "What's all this commotion about?" he said.

"It's just the Silly Sisters!" Lulu said.

"It's just the Silly Sisters!" Mimi repeated.

And they both giggled and giggled.